NICKETTY-NACKETTY
NOO-NOO-NOO

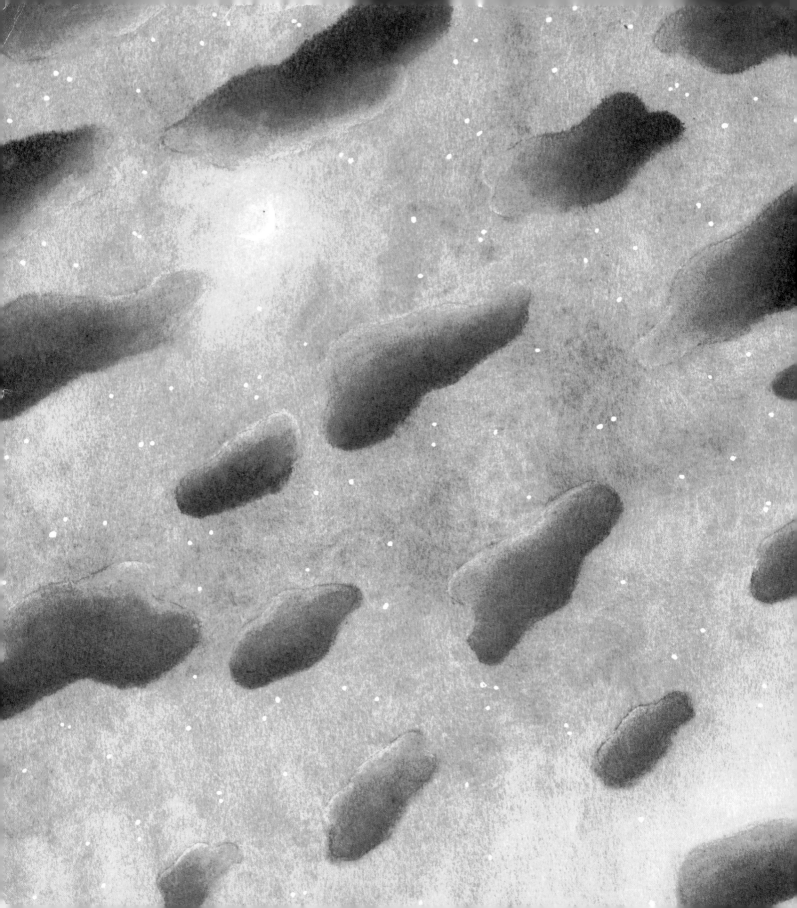

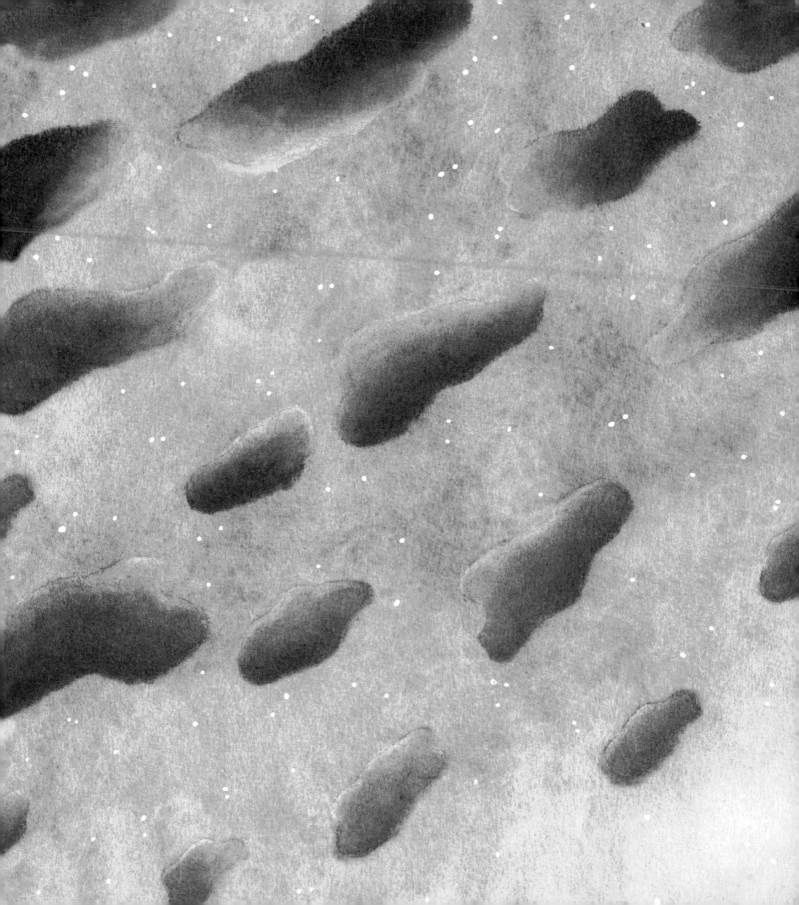

NICKETTY-NACKETTY NOO-NOO-NOO

by Joy Cowley
illustrated by Tracey Moroney

Published in the United States of America in 1998
by MONDO Publishing
First published in New Zealand in 1996
by Scholastic New Zealand Limited

Text copyright © 1996 by Joy Cowley
Illustrations copyright © 1996 by Tracey Moroney

For information contact:
MONDO Publishing
One Plaza Road
Greenvale, New York 11548
Visit our web site at http://www.mondopub.com

Printed in Hong Kong
First Mondo Printing, June 1998
98 99 00 01 02 03 04 05   9 8 7 6 5 4 3 2 1

Library of Congress Cataloging-in-Publication Data
Cowley, Joy.
    Nicketty-nacketty, noo-noo-noo / by Joy Cowley ; illustrated by
Tracey Moroney.
        p.   cm.
    Summary: A swamp orge captures a wee wishy woman and forces
her to make him a good tasty stew, but she tricks him by making it out
of glue.
    ISBN 1-57255-558-0 (pbk. : alk. paper)
    [1. Ghouls and ogres—Fiction. 2. Stories in rhyme.] I. Moroney,
Tracey, ill. II. Title.
PZ8.3.C8345Ni   1999
[E]—dc21   98-17759
                                                                    CIP
                                                                    AC

There once was an ogre called Gobbler Magoo
who lived in a swamp where the wild weeds grew.
Nicketty-nacketty, noo-noo-noo.

A wee wishy woman in an apron of blue,
with her pots and her kettle, was traveling through.
Nicketty-nacketty, noo-noo-noo.

The ogre jumped out and yelled, "Who are you?"
She said, "I'm the maker of good tasty stew."
Nicketty-nacketty, noo-noo-noo.

The ogre then grabbed her and bellowed, "You'll do!
You'll stay here forever and cook me good stew."
Nicketty-nacketty, noo-noo-noo.

He took the wee woman, and all her pots too,
to his moldy old kitchen to make him some stew.
Nicketty-nacketty, noo-noo-noo.

She sliced and she chopped for a moment or two.
Then she filled up a pot with a good tasty brew.
Nicketty-nacketty, noo-noo-noo.

"Hurry! I'm hungry," cried Gobbler Magoo.
The wee woman smiled and tapped her wee shoe.
Nicketty-nacketty, noo-noo-noo.

At last all the cooking and stirring was through.
The ogre sat down with his pot full of stew.
Nicketty-nacketty, noo-noo-noo.

He ate with a spoon and his five fingers too,
while the wee woman watched him shovel and chew.
Nicketty-nacketty, noo-noo-noo.

Then the chewing got slow and the ogre cried, "Ooh!
My teeth seem to stick to this good tasty stew."
Nicketty-nacketty, noo-noo-noo.

The wee woman laughed and said, "That is true.
The stew's thick and tasty. I cooked it in glue!"
Nicketty-nacketty, noo-noo-noo.

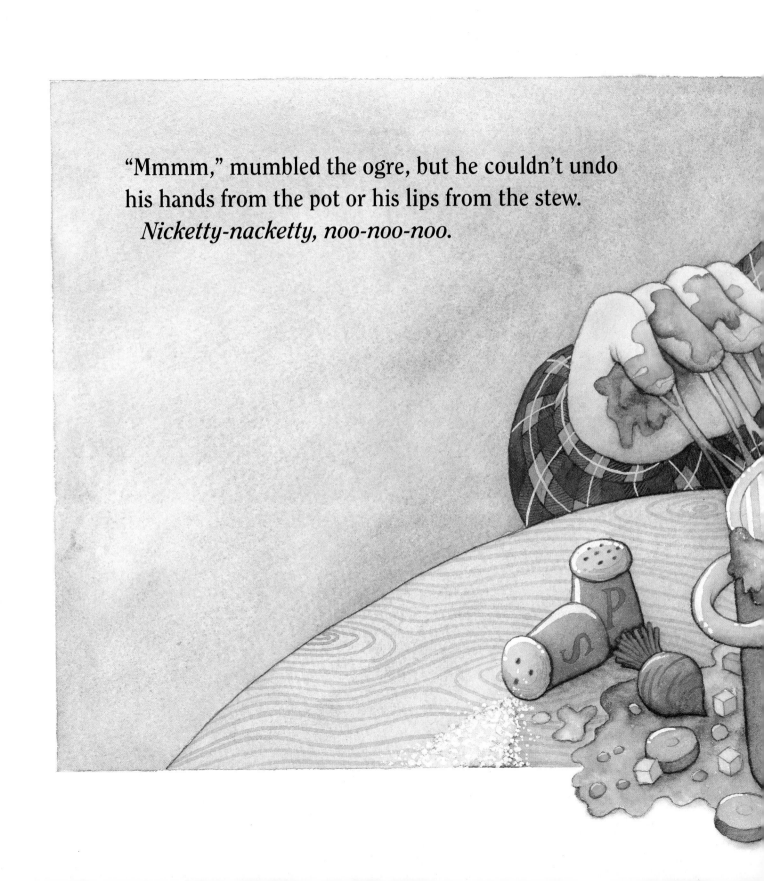

"Mmmm," mumbled the ogre, but he couldn't undo
his hands from the pot or his lips from the stew.
Nicketty-nacketty, noo-noo-noo.

Then the wee wishy woman in her apron of blue
packed her pots and her kettle and said, "Adieu!"
to the stuck-up old ogre who was all in a stew.
Nicketty-nacketty, noo-noo-noo.

Maybe we'll see her as she passes through
with her pots and her pans and her kettle of glue.
But I don't want to eat her stew. Do you?
Nicketty-nacketty, noo-noo-noo.

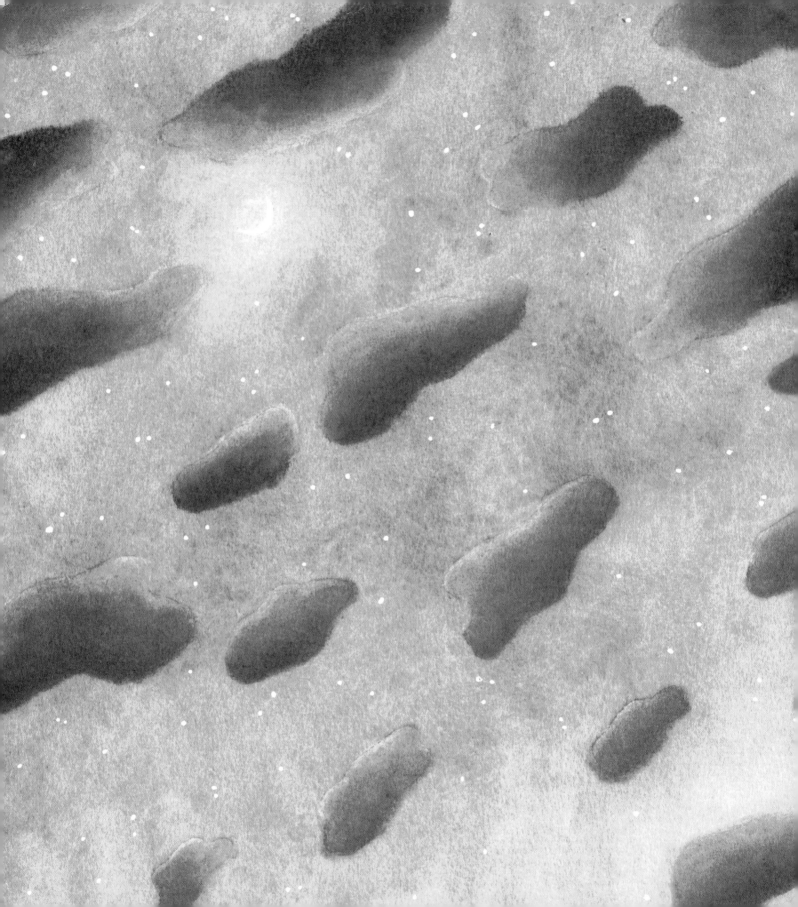

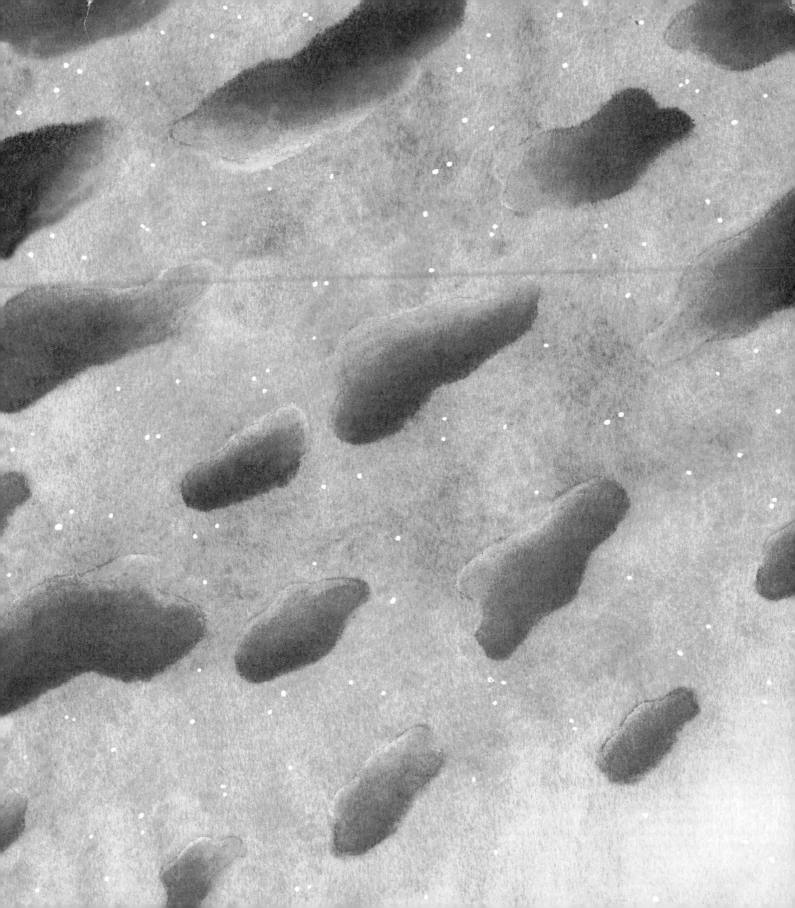